PUFFIN B

BURNT SAUSAGES

The birthday chart is always the focus of Class 4. Everyone looks forward to standing next to it and telling their friends and Mrs Jordan just what they did on their birthday and what was special about it.

Nicola is fed up with hearing Clare boast about the terrific birthday she'd had, so she announces that *hers* will be the most exciting ever! But how can she and her twin brother Mark dream up such a very special birthday when all they have planned is a trip to the park?

In the second story, Neil finds it very difficult living with his brothers and sisters because there is never anywhere he can find to play on his own. He wants somewhere private, his own small place. He is determined to find one or make one – however difficult!

Burnt Sausages and Custard and *No Room for Neil* appear for the first time in one volume.

Marjorie Newman trained as a teacher in London and taught for several years in a local primary school. She lives in Hampshire.

BURNT SAUSAGES
AND CUSTARD

by
Marjorie Newman

Illustrated by Catherine Bradbury

PUFFIN BOOKS

PUFFIN BOOKS

Published by the Penguin Group
27 Wrights Lane, London w8 5TZ, England
Viking Penguin Inc., 40 West 23rd Street, New York, New York 10010, USA
Penguin Books Australia Ltd, Ringwood, Victoria, Australia
Penguin Books Canada Ltd, 2801 John Street, Markham, Ontario, Canada L3R 1B4
Penguin Books (NZ) Ltd, 182–190 Wairau Road, Auckland 10, New Zealand

Penguin Books Ltd, Registered Offices: Harmondsworth, Middlesex, England

Burnt Sausages and Custard first published by
Hamish Hamilton Children's Books 1985
A Room for Neil first published by
Hamish Hamilton Children's Books 1986
Published in one volume in Puffin Books 1988
1 3 5 7 9 10 8 6 4 2

Copyright © Marjorie Newman, 1985, 1986
Illustrations copyright © Catherine Bradbury, 1985, 1986
All rights reserved

Made and printed in Great Britain by
Richard Clay Ltd, Bungay, Suffolk
Filmset in Baskerville

Contents

BURNT SAUSAGES
AND CUSTARD

Chapter One

"*Happy Birthday to you,*
Happy Birthday to you.
Happy Birthday, dear Peter,
Happy Birthday to you!"
sang most of Class 4.

Nicola sang her own words.
"*Happy birthday to you,*
With dumplings and stew.
Burnt sausages and custard,
Happy birthday to you!"

She sang quietly, so that Mrs Jordan wouldn't notice.

Mrs Jordan had just made a new Birthday Chart for Class 4. Peter was the first person to stand beside it while Class 4 sang to him. Then he showed them his birthday cards, and

Ann
Clare
David
Emma
Harriet
Ian
James
Fiona
Lee
Mark
Nico
Oliver
Peter
Roger
Susan
Tony

told them about the special film he'd been to see.

Nicola liked Peter. She liked nearly all the children in Class 4. So it was rather a pity *Clare* had to sit opposite her.

Clare was new that term; and she always seemed to be showing off, or trying to quarrel.

Peter sat down, and Class 4 got on with their work. Nicola was still looking at the chart.

"Mark!" she said. Mark was her twin brother. They sat next to each other.

"What?" said Mark.

"Our birthday's the day before half-term!"

"I know." Mark went on with his

writing. "It's the same day Mrs Jordan's leaving," he muttered.

Nicola knew how he felt. *She* didn't want Mrs Jordan to leave, either. She sighed, and picked up her pencil.

"You're doing that maths all wrong!" hissed Clare. "*I'll* show you. I always get mine right!"

"*I* can do it!" snapped Nicola. She bent low over her work. She found her mistake, and put it right.

"Anyway," said Clare, "my birthday comes before yours."

"We know," said Mark. Funny, thought Nicola. Even *Mark* got cross with Clare. It was something about the way she said things . . .

Clare was talking again.

"I always get piles of presents! And

I always do something special on my birthday."

"So do we!" cried Nicola.

As soon as she'd said it, she wished she hadn't. On their birthday they usually played some games, and had whatever they chose for tea. You couldn't exactly call it *special* . . . And they had about three presents each.

It might have been different if they'd had a dad. But they didn't.

Clare was looking at Nicola's face.

"I bet you don't do anything special at all!" she said. Nicola couldn't bear it.

"I bet we do!" she said.

"Nicola! Clare!" Mrs Jordan had noticed them. "What's the matter?"

Clare answered.

"Nicola says she's doing something special on her birthday!"

It seemed to Nicola that all Class 4 stopped work to listen. She felt her face go red. But Mrs Jordan only said, "I daresay everyone is doing something special on their birthday. And if anyone has time to waste," she added, looking round at Class 4, "I can give them some more work to do. Birthdays or not."

Hastily, Class 4 bent over their books. Nicola tried to get on with her maths. Perhaps Clare would forget what Nicola had said . . .

But Clare didn't forget. Every time she wanted to make Nicola cross, she would say, "Birthday!" It always worked. Nicola always *did* get cross.

"Don't take any notice of her," Mark said to Nicola. "No one else takes any notice of Clare! It doesn't matter what she says!"

But it did matter. And every time someone else stood by the Birthday Chart, and told Class 4 all about their birthday, it mattered more.

Nicola didn't *want* to be different. She wanted their birthday to be as special as everyone else's.

She'd just have to *think* of something . . .

Chapter Two

Nicola thought and thought. She was still trying to think of something when it was James's birthday. He stood by the Chart, and told Class 4 about his new racing pigeon. James knew a lot about racing pigeons. Class 4 were very interested. They asked a lot of questions. Then they wrote about pigeons, and drew pictures of them.

Nicola was working happily. Then Clare said, "I suppose you're going racing for your birthday!"

"What if we are?" said Mark. Nicola pretended not to be listening.

"Why won't you tell?" asked Clare. Mark didn't answer.

"You can't!" said Clare. "Because nothing's going to happen!"

"Wait and see, then!" cried Nicola, joining in after all.

"I will!" said Clare, looking Nicola in the eye.

The next birthday was Emma's.

"I'm going to stay one night with my Gran," Emma told Class 4. "She's going to take me to the ballet."

Nicola wished they had a gran to go and stay with. But they hadn't. She tried to think if there was anyone *else* they could go and stay with . . .

There wasn't.

On their way home through the allotments, Mark said, "Why don't we ask Mum? There might be something special, and she hasn't told us, because it's a surprise."

"Oh yes!" cried Nicola. That could be it! Maybe Mum *did* have a surprise for them!

When tea was over, and they were all doing the washing-up together, Nicola took a deep breath. Then she asked, "Mum, what's happening for our birthday?"

Mum turned to look at them.

"Goodness! It's not your birthday yet, is it?"

"Three weeks," said Mark. Sadly, Nicola put the knives and forks away. There wasn't any surprise . . .

"We could have a picnic in the park," Mum said.

Nicola and Mark looked at each other. A picnic in the park! *That* wasn't special. But Mum was busily finishing washing the pots and pans. She didn't notice anything.

"Decide who you want to invite. Make it two each. O.K.?"

Before they could answer, she went on, "Look at the *time*! I've *got* to get the ironing done tonight. Mark, dear, put the ironing board up for me, will you?"

"Yes," said Mark, sadly.

Back in the living room again, Nicola looked at Mark.

"Nothing," she said.

"*And* Mrs Jordan's leaving," said Mark. "Everything's *rotten!*"

"I *will* think of something!" Nicola declared.

Chapter Three

Clare stood by the Birthday Chart while Class 4 sang the birthday song.

"Burnt sausages and custard . . ." sang Nicola. But it was no fun.

Clare held up what seemed like fifty-dozen birthday cards from her relations. She talked about each one of them. She talked in a showing-off kind of way. Class 4 fidgeted.

They stopped fidgeting when she told them about her presents.

"My mum's given me a portable television set, to go in my bedroom. Gran and Grandad are giving me some video-games. We're going down town to get them, after school today. And we're going into a café, and I can have as many milk-shakes as I like!"

She looked straight at Nicola. Nicola looked down at the table.

"And this is what else I had!" said Clare. She picked up a huge carrier bag, and started to get out her presents one at a time.

"Lovely, Clare," said Mrs Jordan. "But I think you'd better wait till playtime to show those."

Clare tossed her head; but she put

the things back into the bag, and came to sit down. She hung the bag on the back of her chair.

Nicola couldn't help looking at it. Clare had a skipping rope in it. Nicola would have liked to have a turn with that . . .

Usually, Clare was on her own at playtimes. Today she had a crowd of Class 4 round her. Nicola looked at them all. Clare was sure not to want *her*. . . So she went over to Mark, and played football with him, instead.

"Clare's birthday's special, all right," Mark said, gloomily.

Nicola kicked the ball very hard, and didn't answer. Their own birthday was just one week away, and she hadn't had *one* good idea yet. She felt sick.

After play Mrs Jordan told Nicola's group they were having cooking that afternoon.

"You've made cakes with cake-mixture," Mrs Jordan said. "Today you're going to make cakes the other way. The way where you weigh out all the ingredients, and do the job properly!"

She was smiling. Nicola smiled too; because she'd suddenly got an idea. She poked Mark.

"What?" asked Mark, crossly.

"I know how to make our birthday special!" she whispered. "*I'll* make the cake!"

"You don't know how to!" said Mark.

"I *will*, when we've practised this afternoon," said Nicola. Mark looked very doubtful.

"You might manage it with a cake-mix," he said. Nicola shook her head. A cake-mix was no good. This birthday cake was going to be special. Huge. Decorated with icing . . .

"Nicola! Wake up!"

Mrs Jordan's voice made her jump.

She picked up her pencil, and started to copy down the recipe from the blackboard.

That afternoon, Nicola's group stood round the cooking table, and took turns with the scales. Nicola waited impatiently.

Then she looked at Mark's bowl. Mark had put the flour in already.

Nicola picked up the bag of flour, and tipped some into her bowl. She guessed when to stop, matching her flour with Mark's. She rubbed the fat into the flour, the way Mrs Jordan had shown them. Then she added the sugar, and the egg, and began to mix; but the mixture wouldn't come right.

"It's too dry!" said Clare. "I know,

because I make cakes at home. I always get it right."

Nicola frowned. She looked round. Mrs Jordan was busy for the moment with the painting group.

Quietly, Nicola went over to the sink in the corner of the room, got some water in a cup, and came back to the cooking table. She tipped some water into her mixing bowl.

Now it mixed. It was a wet, soggy mixture that stuck to her fingers.

"More flour!" whispered Mark. Quickly, Nicola tipped in some flour. It was too much . . . She *knew* it was too much . . . She wanted to cry. She added some more water from the cup.

"Nicola Jones, what *are* you doing?"

Mrs Jordan had noticed. Nicola's face went red.

"It wouldn't mix," she said.

Mrs Jordan took a good look at the mixing bowl, and at the cup of water. Nicola could see that Mrs Jordan knew *exactly* what she'd been doing.

"All right," Mrs Jordan said. "We'll cook your cakes, Nicola. Then everyone can learn why it's better to follow a recipe carefully!"

Clare grinned. Nicola wanted to hit her.

The cakes smelt beautiful while they were cooking. As soon as they were done, the cooking group shared them out among the class. Mark's were quite nice.

Clare's were perfect.

Nicola's were heavy and doughy. No one could eat them — not even Nicola, although she tried to. Some of Class 4 teased her. Nicola got angry, and Mrs Jordan made them leave her alone. But on the way home, she cried; because she certainly wouldn't try to make a birthday cake . . . She might *never* try to make a cake again.

That night, she had some horrible dreams. All about special birthdays.

She dreamt she and Mark flew to the moon in a space-capsule. They wore space suits; but instead of helmets they had party hats on their

heads. Everyone laughed at them —
and she couldn't breathe . . .

She half woke up, and pushed the
bedclothes away from her face. Then
she slept again. This time she dreamt
Mum had given them a pony for a
special present. It was in the flat.
Nicola wanted to go for a ride on it, so
she tried to get it into the lift. The
pony was too heavy for the lift.
Suddenly Nicola was falling, falling
. . . She called out; and woke herself
up.

Mark said sleepily, "What's the
matter?"

Then Mum came into the bedroom.

"Nicola! Was that you?"

Nicola began to cry.

Mum switched on the light. She came and sat on Nicola's bed, and smoothed the hair from Nicola's forehead.

"What's wrong?" she asked. She looked worried. Nicola couldn't say anything. She was crying too much. Mum hugged her. Mark said,

"It could be about our birthday."

"What d'you mean?" asked Mum. "I thought we'd settled that!"

Nicola struggled to speak.

"It's got to be sp-special!" she sobbed.

"Special?" Mum still didn't understand. Mark told her the whole story. And before he reached the end, he'd begun to cry, too.

"We stand by the chart," he

finished, "and *everyone* has had something special to tell! Everyone!"

"Especially Clare!" sobbed Nicola.

Mum looked very sad. "Twins, of
course I want your birthday to be
special. But you know there isn't any
money to spare! I'm sure you're making too much fuss about this,
anyway."

Nicola tried to stop crying; but she couldn't.

"You've got yourself into a proper state!" scolded Mum.

"She's been worrying for ages," said Mark. "Ever since she told Clare."

38

"Clare! She's the one nobody will play with, isn't she? Unless she lets them borrow her toys?"

Nicola had never thought of that; but it was true. Clare didn't have any friends . . .

"It's not just Clare," Mark said. "*Everybody* has a special time on their birthday."

"And you don't want to be different." Mum understood at last. She sighed.

"Put something warm on, and come out to the kitchen. We'll have a talk."

Chapter Four

Sitting in the kitchen, drinking hot cocoa, Nicola felt a lot better.

"Look," said Mum, "maybe we could *make* the picnic special."

Mark said, "If we have it on Saturday afternoon — the day after our birthday — the band will be playing."

"Great!" nodded Mum. "Pity we

can't invite the band to your party!"
she added.

Mum was joking; but Mark said
slowly, "If we could invite somebody
special . . . like the Queen . . ."

And suddenly, Nicola knew what to
do.

"Ask Mrs Jordan!" she cried.

Mark began to smile a huge smile.

Mum said, "You can't ask her just
because she would make your birthday special for you!"

"It's not just that," Mark muttered
shyly. "We like her — and she's
leaving."

"Please, Mum, please!" begged
Nicola.

"Can we do the invitation now?"
asked Mark.

"I think I'll put in a little note, as well," said Mum.

On their birthday morning, the twins stood by the Chart while Class 4 sang to them. Then Nicola took a deep breath, and looked straight at Clare.

"For our birthday," she said, "we are having a picnic in the park — and Mrs Jordan is coming!"

Class 4 didn't believe it. Mrs Jordan nodded.

"Quite true! It's tomorrow afternoon. And, Nicola, I hope there won't be any burnt sausages and custard!"

Class 4 laughed. Nicola's face went red. Mrs Jordan had known about that all the time . . . but she was smiling; so it was all right.

Clare was very quiet.

It was sad that afternoon, when everyone went into the hall to give Mrs Jordan some flowers, and a good-bye present.

But next day, Mark, Nicola and

Mum took the party things to the park. Mrs Jordan — and Mr Jordan — were waiting for them. They found a good place near the band, and settled down. Then someone called, "Hi!"

It was Clare, with her mother, coming across the grass.

"Oh no!" groaned Nicola.

"Ssh!" said Mum. And Mrs Jordan said, "I think Clare's lonely. I believe she'd like to be friends, but she doesn't quite know how to tell you."

Nicola was very surprised. Before

she could answer, Mark cried, "Look!"

Coming across the grass now were nearly all the children from Class 4; and lots of their relations. Nearly everyone had brought a card for the twins, as well as their own picnic tea.

"Good gracious!" said the bandmaster. "This must be the biggest birthday party ever!"

And he made the band play "Happy Birthday to You!"

"Burnt sausages and custard . . ." sang Mrs Jordan. Nicola couldn't believe her ears!

She grinned at Clare. Clare grinned back. The band played again; and suddenly, everyone was dancing, on the grass, in the sunshine.

A ROOM FOR NEIL

Chapter One

It was Saturday morning.

Neil peeped round the door of the sitting-room. Great! No one was in there. He'd be able to paint in peace.

Happily, Neil went over to the table. He put down the paper, the paint-brushes and the paint-box. The paint-box was one of his best things. It had tubes of paint, as well as ordinary powder ones.

He went out to the kitchen. Mum gave him the saucers he used for mixing paint on. He found a jar for the painting water.

When he got back to the sitting-room, his two-year-old sister Louise was there. She was climbing on to a chair by the table. She was holding one of his paint-brushes.

"What are you doing?" cried Neil.

"Paint!" smiled Louise.

She began to spread newspaper over the table.

"You can't use *my* paints!" cried Neil. Louise still mixed up the colours, so that everything came out muddy brown.

"Paint!" said Louise again. She was going to cry any minute.

"Oh – all right," said Neil, crossly. He gave her one piece of paper. He squeezed some red paint on to a saucer.

"You use that paint!" he said. "And *only* that!"

"Red!" smiled Louise.

Neil settled to work. He started a space-ship. It was going to be super . . .

The door opened. In rushed James. James was eight, one year older than Neil.

"Have you seen my football?" he asked.

"No," said Neil.

"Nope," said Louise. She was painting huge red crosses on her paper.

James looked at Neil's painting.

"What's *that*?" he asked.

"It's a space-ship!" said Neil.

"It looks like a sick tortoise to me," said James. He rushed off.

Crossly, Neil painted over his space-ship until it was a blob. It could probably be turned into a mountain, or something . . .

His big sister Marie came in.

"Neil!" she cried. "You don't scrub like that with a paint-brush! I'll show you."

She tried to take the brush from him.

"Leave it!" cried Neil. "I know how to do it!"

"All right!" Marie was surprised at Neil's quick temper. "Louise – shall I do a lady dancing for you?"

Louise nodded.

"They're *my* paints!" Neil said. But Marie and Louise didn't even hear him.

Angrily, Neil started to load his things on to a tray.

"Give us a bit of black before you go," said Marie. She helped herself, squeezing some paint on to the saucer.

Neil was so angry, he couldn't speak. He picked up the tray, and stomped out of the room. Where could he go?

He stomped into the dining-room.

"Neil! Is that you?" called Mum, from the kitchen. "Don't settle there, dear. It's nearly lunch-time. Lay the table, please."

Neil sighed. It was his week for

laying the table. He put his tray of things carefully on to the wide windowsill, and went out to the kitchen. He got the plastic table-cloth from the drawer. When he came back to the sitting-room the cat was treading round and round on his painting paper. She was making herself a cosy place to sleep.

"No!" yelled Neil. "Get off!"

The cat blinked at him. Then she sat down anyway.

Neil banged the cloth on to the table. Mum came to the door.

"Whatever's wrong?" she asked.

"Well!" said Neil. "There's absolutely nowhere at *all* for me to do my things!"

Mum looked sad.

"I wish you could all have a room of your own," she said. "But with four children, a cat, a dog, Dad, and me – and a not-very-big house – we just have to learn to share."

She went back to the kitchen.

Angrily, Neil went on laying the table. If only he could *think* of something ... Somewhere to go ... Somewhere to be private, and on his own ...

Chapter Two

While Neil was eating stew and dumplings, he had an idea.

As soon as the meal was over, he ran out into the garden. Fido the dog ran out behind him. Fido's tail was wagging. His eyes were bright.

"No, no! I didn't come out here to play with you, Fido," Neil told him crossly.

Fido's ears went down. His tail drooped.

"Oh, all right," said Neil. He threw Fido's ball several times. Then he ran indoors.

"Mum! Please can I have an old sheet, or something, to make a tent in the garden?" he asked.

"A tent! This time of year!" said Mum.

"Please!" begged Neil. Mum looked at him. Then she said,

"There's an old blanket in the cupboard. Put a coat on, mind!"

"Thanks, Mum!" cried Neil.

He got the blanket, and some string, and ran out into the garden. Fido chased after him, tugging at the blanket.

"Drop it, you silly dog!" said Neil.
Fido let go. Neil laid the blanket
out flat. Then he lifted one corner,
and tied it to the hedge, as high as he
could reach. He tied up another corner. Then he stretched the blanket
down to the ground, and weighted the
edge with big stones. It made a lean-
to.

He had to hitch the top edge over pieces of twig, here and there; but he managed it in the end.

He went indoors for his coat. He borrowed an old mac of Mum's, as well. He draped the mac over one end of the lean-to. The other end was near the house wall; so the tent was private. He used a plastic sack for the floor. Then Neil fetched his painting things and went into his tent. Great!

Somewhere private, at last!

He set to work.

He'd been painting for about five minutes, when he heard James outside. He knew it was James. Only James kicked a football against the house wall.

"Goal!" yelled James.

"Woof! Woof!" barked Fido.

Next second, Neil's tent caved in on top of him. The ball had bounced on to the blanket. Fido had bounced on to the blanket, as well.

For a moment, there was a struggling heap. Neil shouted,

"Ugh! James! Get him off!" as loudly as he could. It wasn't very loud, because he was nearly smothered by the blanket.

James laughed so much, he could hardly help. But in the end he pulled Fido off. Neil struggled to his feet. His tent was broken. His painting was ruined.

In between laughing, James said, "What a stupid place to be painting in!"

"Stupid yourself!" shouted Neil. "It was my private tent, and you've ruined it!"

"Sorry," said James. He looked surprised because Neil was making such a fuss. "Anyway," he said, "it's starting to rain."

It was.

James and Fido went in. Neil would have to go in, too.

Sadly, he wrapped himself in

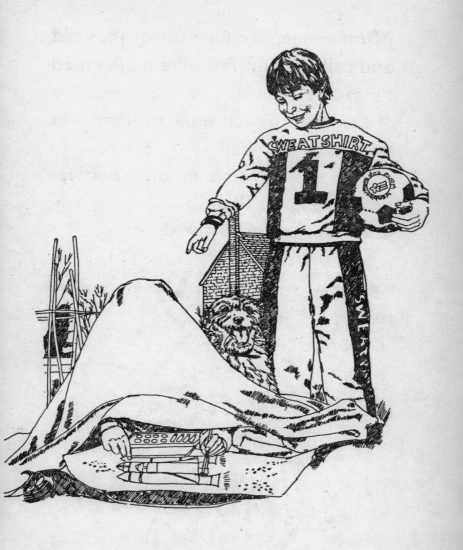

Mum's mac. He took down the tent, and collected everything into the plastic sack.

Loaded, he stumbled along the path past the shed.

The shed! Wait a minute! Perhaps he could go in there!

He pushed open the door.

Chapter Three

There wasn't a lot of room in the shed. Dad was keen on do-it-yourself. He stored lots of tools, and pieces of wood, and nails and screws in there. The shed was also cold, and rather dark, on a day like this. But it *was* private.

Neil dumped the sack on the floor. He began to unpack the things.

The painting paper was crumpled and dirty. The water-jar had upset long ago. Anyway, Neil didn't feel like painting now . . .

Perhaps he could get one of his jigsaw puzzles . . . or a book . . .

While he was thinking, Neil started to untangle the string he'd used to make the tent. He began to wind it into a neat ball. And he had an idea!

At the same moment, Mum opened the back door, and called to him.

"Neil! Do come in! It's so damp out there!"

"O.K.," he shouted back, quite cheerfully. He'd been going to go indoors, anyway, for his new idea. He packed up the things again, and went into the kitchen.

"Good boy," said Mum. She smoothed his hair as he passed her. He dodged away – although really he liked it when she did that.

He put the blanket and the mac away. Then he hurried up to his bedroom. He dumped the sack and the painting things on his bed, and set to work.

He had to share this room with

James – but half of it *was* Neil's. He already *had* a space of his own – only nobody noticed it. Now they would see it quite clearly.

Neil found some of James' left-over drawing pins on the windowsill. He picked up the string, and pinned one end of it to the top of his bedside table. Then he stretched the string out across the middle of the room, and pinned the other end to the top of the chest-of-drawers. Great! The string made a sort of fence. Good job James had the bed near the door! Neil's bed was along the wall by the side window.

He found a piece of paper, and wrote PRIVATE! KEEP OUT! in very large letters.

He was hanging the paper over the string when Mum came into the room.

"What's all this?" she asked.

"I've marked my half of the room," said Neil.

"Don't be silly, Neil!" she said. "You can't have a piece of string across the room like that! Louise

could hurt herself. And Fido will keep
tugging at it. He'll pull the table over!
And how am I supposed to get
by? . . . You'll have to take it down.
At once!"

"But Mum –" said Neil.

"NOW!" said Mum.

Sadly, Neil unpinned the string.

"Look," said Mum, "you can lay
out your string along the floor. That
will mark out your space just as well."

"All right," sighed Neil.

Mum went downstairs. Neil laid

the string along the middle of the
floor. He took a long time arranging
it. Perhaps it *would* do just as well . . .

Marie came in.

"Neil – you know your junk collection? Have you got any beads in it?
Jenny's just come over. She's making
a belt, and she's going to show me
how to do it."

Neil couldn't believe his eyes! Marie had walked right across his string, without even noticing it! She was looking in his junk-box!

Fido came bustling in, tail wagging. His feet sent the string all ways.

"He's been looking for you," said Marie. Fido jumped on to Neil's bed.

"That's *my* bed! Get off!" cried Neil. Marie looked at him in surprise.

"You've never minded him on your bed before," she said.

"Well, I do now!" said Neil. He pulled Fido off. "And I don't collect beads!" he added.

"I don't know what's got into you," said Marie. She went away. Fido followed her.

Neil lay on his bed, staring up at

the ceiling. Everything was *hopeless*.
He'd *never* have a place of his own . . .
Somewhere where all his things
would be safe, and he could work in
peace . . .

The cat walked silently into the
room. She jumped up beside him.

"This is my bed, not yours!" he
said. He smoothed her; but she was
cross. She jumped down, and went in
under the bed.

"It's a pity I can't sit under there, too," thought Neil. He thought a bit more. "The bed's too low. That's why I can't sit under there comfortably. There's a lot of space, otherwise . . ."

He rolled over, off, and in beside the cat. He lay looking up at the underside of his bed. Yes! That was it! If Dad could —

At that moment, he heard the front door bang. Dad was home from work.

Neil rolled out from under the bed, and rushed down the stairs.

"Dad! Dad!" he yelled. "I've had an idea! Can you come?"

Dad was still taking off his coat. Mum said,

"*Now* what, Neil?"

"Come and see! Upstairs!" said Neil.

The whole family had arrived, to see what all the noise was about; so everyone followed Neil upstairs.

Neil explained. Dad said,

"Well –"

Mum said,

"I wish you would!" and gave Dad one of her special looks.

"All right," said Dad. "I'll have a go!"

"Great!" cried Neil. "When can we start?"

"Mind if I have tea first?" teased Dad.

Chapter Four

It was Monday evening before Neil
and Dad could really get going. The
work took them two weeks. By then,
Neil's bed was standing on very tall
legs. He could stand up straight
underneath it. At each end were sets
of drawers. They made the whole
thing stronger, *and* gave Neil plenty of
space for his things.

Dad fixed a small ladder so that
Neil could climb up into bed; and put
a small rail so that Neil wouldn't fall
out. Mum gave Neil some net cur-
tains to pin along the side of the bed,
making a front wall for his room. And
she gave him a mat for his floor.

The side window was just right for
daylight; and Marie and James
bought him a huge torch, in case he
needed more light in the evenings.

The lower rungs of the ladder made
a hole which Neil could use as a door.
He had a piece of card fixed to it, on
hinges made of string.

When it was finished, everyone
came to look at it. They liked it.
Louise started to go in, but Mum and

Dad both said, "NO!" very loudly, both together.

"This is Neil's private room!" Dad said, very firmly. "Do you all understand?"

Everybody did – even Fido. The cat pretended she wasn't bothered anyway.

The family went away. Happily, Neil went into his room. At last!

Somewhere private, his own place.

Every day for the next week he made his own bed, and swept his own floor, as he had promised Mum. He sorted out all his toys, and other belongings, and arranged the drawers neatly. He sat and painted, or drew, or did his puzzles, or made his junk models, or read his books.

No one came bursting in. No one touched any of his things. After a while, they seemed to forget he was there.

Neil sat in his room. He heard James, Marie and Louise playing together on the landing. He heard James chasing Marie because she'd taken his coloured pencils. He heard

them laughing together. He heard
Louise playing with Fido. And he
sighed.

He went on with his own things.
He heard Mum and Louise laughing
and talking together. He heard Dad
talking to the cat. He sighed.

He heard Marie and Jenny playing
together. He sighed deeply, and went
on drawing.

Then he sat and thought. Of course, it *was* great to have a place of his own . . . He sighed again . . . Just at the moment, he couldn't think of anything he wanted to get on with . . .

Next day, Neil set out one of James' favourite games. Then he went downstairs. James was hanging around in the kitchen.

"Want to come and play with me?" Neil asked. "In my room?"

"O.K.," said James.

Happily, Neil let James into his room. He showed him all the things he'd done. They played a game together. Then James went away.

Cheerfully, Neil packed up. Tomorrow, he might invite Louise in.

Or Marie. Or his friend Andrew. He
might invite them – or he might not.
It was up to him.

And it felt great!

THE RAILWAY CAT'S SECRET
Phyllis Arkle

Stories about Alfie, the Railway Cat, and his sworn enemy, Hack the porter. Alfie tries to win over Hack by various means with often hilarious results.

WORD PARTY
Richard Edwards

A delightful collection of poems – lively, snappy and easy to read.

THE THREE AND MANY WISHES OF JASON REID
Hazel Hutchins

Jason is eleven and a very good thinker, so when he is granted three wishes he is very wary indeed. After all, he knows the tangles that happen in fairy stories!

THE AIR-RAID SHELTER
Jeremy Strong

Adam and his sister Rachel find a perfect place for their secret camp in the grounds of a deserted house, until they are discovered by their sworn enemies and things go from bad to worse.

RED LETTER DAY
Alexa Romanes

It was meant to be such a very special day in the village, but it did seem at one time as if the whole thing would end in disaster ...

SUN AND RAIN
Ann Ruffell

The heatwave seemed to go on for ever, but with the help of a rain-making kit Susan managed to produce a solitary rain cloud.

THE RELUCTANT DRAGON
Kenneth Grahame

The Boy was not at all surprised to find a Dragon on the South Downs, but he was surprised to find that it was so civilized.

HANK PRANK AND HOT HENRIETTA
Jules Older

Hank and his hot-tempered sister, Henrietta, are always getting themselves into trouble, but the doings of this terrible pair make for an entertaining series of adventures.

MR MAJEIKA AND THE HAUNTED HOTEL
Humphrey Carpenter

Class Three of St Barty's are off on an outing to Hadrian's Wall with their teacher Mr Majeika (who also happens to be a magician).

Stranded in the fog when the tyres of their coach are mysteriously punctured, they take refuge in a nearby hotel called the Green Banana. Soon some very spooky things start to happen. Strange lights, ghostly sounds and vanishing people . . .

NO PRIZE OR PRESENTS FOR SAM
Thelma Lambert

Sam just has to find a pet to enter in the Most Unusual Pets Competition at the village fête. But the animal he chooses leads to some very unexpected publicity! When Sam decides he'll give his Aunty and Uncle a happy Christmas, the only problem is how can he earn some money?

These two entertaining stories about Sam's ingenuity and determination appear in one volume for the first time.

THE HICCUPS AT NO. 13
Gyles Brandreth

The Brown family are looking forward to a relaxing Sunday morning, but when Hamlet has the hiccups nobody is safe. There's chaos in the kitchen and disaster at the doctors . . .